KIAMANI ROBEY

Shea Butter Rocks

A Love and Butter Love Story

Contents

Prologue

In the beginning there was a pen, paper and a dream to write a short story. I created short story after short story, but could not determine if I wanted to connect their passions, their dreams, and/or their visions. I tried to decide if I would take one short story and conjure its long present and future, but decided it was only worthy of its short space. So I created a character so unique, so normal, so likable, so free that reminding me of a flower in Spring. The rains would pour, the winds would push her around, but she continued to grow. She had the wings of a butterfly, but the strength of an eagle, seeking and flying about. She was surrounded by love ones with different personalities and motives that gave her a run for her money. But while she learned lessons and went about her daily life, she was startled by a lion's strength while being mesmerized by his charm. And there her journey begins and also where Shea Butter Rocks takes form.

But without further ado, I introduce, Jasmine.

The Scent Had Me at, "Hello."

* * *

As I walked down the sandy walk way to the beach, a fine, chocolate specimen came into view. He was no ordinary man. No, he was chiseled and glowing. Not that playing in your mother's makeup kind of glow, that sun-kissed the gods kind of illumination. He didn't just captivate me, he made most woman gawk at his broad shoulders, his full beard, and his swag so fierce. But I wasn't aware of all of that. I had seen the light shimmer of the beautiful Adonis that was before me. He smelled of rich cocoa and a hint of spice. Yes, he was killing the game and didn't even know it. I saw in his hand a jar of my favorite Body Butter from the line: Deep Earth. Yeah, I use *Simple, Delish!* products, but Deep Earth and *Simple, Delish!* are married in my book. Intertwined with love and whipped with delicious scents. Yeah, he was my kind of man. Dripping in body butter and positive aura. How could I ask for more? Well...."*BEEP, BEEP!*" My alarm went off for the last time before I scurried off to the shower. I had a big day ahead of me. Client conversations, meetings with my folks and a lunch with my favorite sister. "One

1

more moment to visualize!" I yelled to no one in particular and smothered my pillow on my face.

I hurried with my briefcase to the boardroom. Five members of the leadership team talked sports as I got situated in my seat. They continued as I allowed a few sips of water to wet my palette. I looked around the room at the flat screen TV and poster-boards that created a unique collage of our past company functions. I looked at my peers as they planned their after work festivities at the local bar. Faces smiled at the picture of a young woman scandalously clad on a phone that was being passed from hand to hand. Someone even offered to pass the phone to me, when I felt a tinge of anger rise within my soul. *How dare they not recognize that I am a member of this professional alliance that topped the numbers monthly? How could they forget beauty was not to passed around as a desert on a menu? How could they continue to converse about where they are going to meet up while still in the meeting?* I counted to ten and remembered the beautiful man from my dreams. I imagined him meeting me for lunch, telling me to pack up and put in my two week notice because he was ready to take me away. I closed my eyes and smiled as well rode off into the sunset...

"Jasmine, enough with the daydreaming. Let's get to business." His look was of greed and dismay as I opened my eyes to the men piercing at me. I shook my head and unpacked my suitcase. *I can't daydream, but you guys can talk about the women you want to meet.* I shook my head. We began to review the minutes of the last meeting and worked through questions pertaining to our client functions. Each member took time to explain their findings of the research they completed and guaranteed to be competitive on the financial front. The time flew as we packed up our things and shook hands. I looked at my watch and began to move swiftly. I did not want to be late. *On to the next meeting of the day, lunch with Mia, my lovely egotistical baby sister*, I thought as I headed for the elevator doors.

"Darling!" She yelled from across the street. I crossed the sidewalk to meet a young woman with a big personality. She was a beautiful friend, a great listener, and a whole lot of fun. "I missed you." We embraced tightly. I smelled the perfume in her hair. She loved to bargain shop, but her perfume was her guilty pleasure. "Expensive in price and in aesthetics", she would say as we window shopped for perfumes monthly. We sat at an open table at a small restaurant in the city. It was one of my favorite places to get a cold brewed ice coffee and a Danish pastry. "How's it been? I've been trying to catch up with you for months." I smiled at Mia, but couldn't shake my prince out of my head. "Girl, I've been doing the usual. Working on projects, while training, while drowning. The corporate way." I laughed. "But I see a diamond I've never seen before. Are you engaged?" My sister smiled a mischievous grin. I hadn't spoken to my sister is a very long time. I usually follow her on social media, but over the last couple of months, she went ghost. Last week, Mia called me in her usual chipper voice, but there was something deeper underneath. I had to meet her. "I might be. But I might just like large diamonds on my ring finger." She waved her left hand in the air. I got up and gave her a hug. I was so excited for her. She went through so much in her early twenties with men that I wasn't sure if she would ever want to experience love again. "Yes, let me tell you how I met him. I was waiting out in the rain for a driver some months ago. I checked for them on my app, but then the car disappeared off the map. I started to scream. I was so angry and it began to rain. I could feel my blood boiling. I left my umbrella in the house and did not want to go back up the steps to get it. Before I could decide if I needed the umbrella, a car pulled up with the taxi sign on. I got in the car without asking any questions. The driver said he was sorry he was late, but he got hemmed up at the light. I gave him a puzzled look because I didn't call a taxi. He asked me where I was going and took me to my destination. Before I got out, he got a call from his original customer asking where he was. He looked back to me and before he could ask me any questions, I left a hundred dollar bill on the seat and hopped out the car. To my disbelief, the driver parked the car and began running behind me. I kept up the speed as long as I could until I was tired. Standing in the rain with no umbrella, the driver caught up to me. I felt his spirit envelope me before I saw his face. He took off his jacket and put it around me. He faced me and looked in my eyes. Something clicked within my heart. I knew I was breaking down. I could feel it coming. And then the water show from within began." My sister sat back in her chair. I could see her eyes water as she recalled the event. I caught hold of her hand and she began her story again. "He drew my pain out of my secret place and all I could do was cry and fold up in his arms. And he held me in the rain for what felt like years even though it was just a couple moments. I looked into his eyes and saw protection. I saw a king that was awaiting his queen and I knew I was the perfect fit. But I also saw pain that had been hidden and locked in barricaded doors. I remembered that I was crying in the arms of a man I did not know and I immediately pushed away from him. I looked back into his eyes and he took both of my hands. He said something I will never forget as if he was reading my mind. *"Those doors are locked for a reason, but for you I will get the healing I need. I want to help you heal, but I can't do that if I am broken."* I sat back in my seat and imagined that night before me. Instead of my sister, I interjected my own lonely body, moistened by the rain. I decided to pull him to me and I felt the heat from his Shea buttered skin when.......*"*Hey you, are you okay?" I opened my eyes to see my sister looking at me intensively. I smiled, but hurried to compose my thoughts. "Sure, I am just so excited for you. I wanted to imagine the whole scene." Mia looked at me as if I was a martian. "No, you were daydreaming again. Haven't we talked about this before. You will never be able to get a man if you are always in that head of yours." I rolled my eyes at my little "Big" sister. She was growing up before my eyes. It was an amazing thing to see. We embraced and began walking toward the street. "Make sure you take time off for the wedding shower, the night out and the wedding itself." She hugged me tighter. I agreed. I looked across the street to my next destination. Getting on the streetcar to meet my mother. I knew this was going to be the most unique of meetings yet. "Chao'." I blew a kiss to Mia as I crossed the sidewalk to the depot. I took a moment to stretch my legs and arms before taking a set on the bench. "Time really flies when you are having fun, ey?" I got out of my head long enough to see the candy dipped man that sat on the bench next to mine. He was clothed in a double-breasted suit, a charming next tie and a baseball cap to match. Yes, he had butter written all over him. And that was the first time I laid my eyes on the chocolate Adonis named Shawn.

Your Not From Around Here, Huh?

* * *

The trolley pulled up at the exact time I caught my breath. He stood about five foot, ten inches tall, with a swag so "hip hop", but an aura of peace and passion. My type of guy. He moved out the way to let me step onto the trolley. I ascended the steps, but managed to fall over the final step. I wobbled until I fell backwards. And who was there to catch me? Well, another woman with a summer dress on because "*hip hop swag*" moved out the way to let another woman get on first. Such a gentleman, *but what about me?* I thanked the lady and began my plight up the stairs again only to have all eyes on me. I sat down in my shame and began to fiddle with my clothes. Before I could begin to dream of another elaborate way to make this a great story out of my mishap, *Mr. Hip-hop Swag* came to my rescue and slid in the seat next to me. He smelled of mint and coconut, from the Deep Earth Mint Wonder line. I inhaled one more time and smiled in his direction. His look was of amazement and puzzlement combined. "That was terrible fall...for that lady who caught you." He began to smile and laugh a hearty laugh. I saw his white teeth. Not a spec of coffee or tea stained his smile.

6

"So, how are you? Are you okay?" He seemed concerned unlike the usual questions people ask for show. "I am okay, I was all in my head and missed the step. Thanks for asking." I sat back in my seat. Mr. *Hip Hop* unbuttoned his jacket, took it off and laid it in his lap. "Now, you didn't answer my question from earlier, did time fly while you were having fun?" I looked at him closely and didn't place the question from before. It finally became aware that he must have been waiting for the shuttle and saw my sister and I having our conversation. "Oh, so you were watching us?" His smile faded as he smoothed his jacket. "I was possibly just taking a look at a beautiful lady that caught my eye. Maybe nothing more, nothing less." He smiled once again and I knew I wanted to play his game. Before I could answer, Mr *Hip Hop* spoke again. "My name is Shawn. And yours?" I shook his hand slowly. "Jasmine, like the flower." He nodded as if he approved. The driver began to advise of the next stops. I pulled the lever to stop the trolley. "My turn." I rose to my feet and grabbed the bar as the trolley came to a stop. "Bye." I smiled as I made my way to the exit door. As I stepped down to the street, Shawn grabbed my arm to assist. "Wouldn't want you to fall like before. My mom would be mad. She didn't raise a gentleman for nothing." He guided me to the safety area as the trolley went on its way. "Thank you, but this was not your stop. The next shuttle is not for thirty minutes." I was concerned and joyed at the same time. "I have time. I would like to walk you to your destination and then I will catch the next one." He gestured that he wanted to carry my bag and I acquiesced. We walked on the street in silence. The sidewalk ended as night fell. "So, Jasmine tell me about yourself." I began to breathe deeply hoping he would not want any deep, dark secrets. It was too early in the game! "Um, let's see. I am a Gemini, I love the color pink, I am great at flying kites and I love tortillas." I could see his eyes light up. "Your a Gemini, huh? Okay, great to know. All lovely things you told me about, thank you. But tell me who you are on the inside. What sets your soul on fire?" A smile plastered my face as I shook my head. He was unique and that was refreshing. I looked up to the sky and screamed as the rain hit my face with force. I was caught in the moment, when Shawn took off his jacket and put it around my shoulders. He put his arm around me and guided me to a store that had an awning. I shook my head and laughed at how absurd the situation was. I was standing under an awning with a gentleman that I did not know, covered by his suit jacket only minutes from my mother's house in the rain. How marvelous was that! But then his phone rang and my energy seeped down the drain with the rain.

Surprise!

* * *

He pulled out his phone and smiled as the number lit up the screen. I could feel heat rising from my inner core. My thoughts began to run wildly. *"I don't even know this man, why am I overreacting?* He spoke softly. I could hear a woman in the background, but could not decipher what she was saying. "No problem. I will be there soon. I just got... turned around. I'm right around the corner." He stuck his phone back in his pocket and turned to me. I could feel my inner child coming out to play. "Turned around huh? Well, I don't want to keep you." I gave Shawn his jacket and walked briskly in the rain towards my mother's house. I didn't turn around to see the confused look on his face. I didn't hear as he caught up with me, this time, walking in silence. He didn't look at me, just kept walking next to me. I didn't notice the look on his face, when I walked to a house that I'd been a million times, and hugged the man who opened the door. I also didn't notice that he pulled his hat down closer to his eyes, stuck his hands in his pocket, looked on with a scowl and walked faster in the rain till I couldn't see his cap.

9

"Uh, what did I do to deserve that?" A tall, middle age man closed the door. "Lana, look what the cat drug in." A tall, statuesque woman came with a hardy smile. "Baby, your all wet. Ronald, get this baby a towel and a blanket." Lana, pulled me near her and hugged me tight. She smelled of fresh, chocolate chip cookies and love. I started to cry. She hugged me tighter, rocking to a song I could not hear. Lana, guided me to the living area as Ronald put the items on the couch. "My Lord, what brings you out here tonight?" Ronald looked at me with concern. I told them everything. About our meeting, the walk, the phone call. Ronald didn't say a word. "Baby, these men out here are different. He may have just wanted to make sure you were safe, have a conversation with you, but nothing more. He may have had a wife." Lana said with a shrug. I recalled the whole time we were around each other. "No, I didn't see a ring." I shook my head. "Well, he had someone. No man is going to answer the phone while in the rain with a pretty woman unless he is with someone or it's his.." Ronald and Lana said it at the same time, "Mama!" They both laughed. I did not find it funny. "Baby, maybe it is all in your head. He was talking to his mother. Did you get his number earlier?" I shook my head no. "Well, maybe you will see him again." Lana nodded as if she was sure of it. "He did look familiar. Are you sure he is not from around here? Ronald pursed his head as if he was thinking. "No, I've never seen him before. Remember, I grew up around here." I rolled my eyes and hugged them both. My phone began to chime. "Mom, hey, I'm right down the street. I got caught in a rain pour. Yeah, are you okay?" My mother sounded upset. She mentioned she wasn't up for company and that something came up. She asked for a rain check. "Sure, no problem. Are you sure you don't want me to come over?" I heard her breathe deeply and could imagine her shrugging, but she said no. "Okay, we can reschedule. I hope you feel better." My mother disconnected the call. "Have you guys heard from my mom? She sounded frustrated." They both shrugged. I sat back down on the couch as Lana went to the kitchen to get tea for us all. "I guess I'm hanging out with you guys." I smiled. Ronald went to the back room as Lana and I drank tea and talked about men. She and Ronald were my godparents. I'd known them since elementary school when my mom and I moved in the area. She needed a baby-sitter and they needed a little girl to spoil. It was a match made in heaven.

I snuggled under a blanket and turned on a movie. It was an old, black and white western. I watched this as a child with Ronald always near. He loved cowboy flicks and always knew all the words. I loved the passion he had for those shows. For Halloween one year, he bought me a cowgirl outfit and we went through town pretending to play out one of his favorite shows *Cops and Robbers*. Those were the days. As I dosed off and my eyes closed, a picture of Shawn flashed before me. His white teeth glimmered as the light in his eyes danced. His face quickly turned melancholy as I woke up from my nightmare. I had to speak to him again to apologize for what I said to him. He did walk me toward my destination and he tried to shield me from the storm. My head began to ache as my mind settled back down. I curled under the blanket and went back to sleep.

A Turn for the Worse or Better. Maybe?

* * *

I could not get him off my mind. I imagined all of his brown skin, bathed in rich, creamy body butter, with a scent that brought my senses to a place of elevation. Yes, I was daydreaming again and loving it! But my boss wasn't so happy about it. I messed up two client meetings, missed a few deadlines and before my boss could put me on a "break", better known as a *leave of good faith*, I found myself going into his office and officially saying, "I quit!" That was the most liberating thing I had ever done and probably the most scary as well. I did not have six months of savings to live on. I wasn't even sure of what I wanted to be when I grew up! And I was grown already! But, I felt it was a great thing at the moment to do. I began packing up my belongings, when a fellow co-worker came to my door. "Leaving so soon?" She smiled as she sat in my chair. "I know, I just couldn't take the stress. I've doing this for so long, I think its time to change the scenery." Marilyn was a great "work" friend that I loved dearly. She always had the right thing to say, at the right time while throwing in humor when she could. "I never thought I'd say goodbye. We were so good together. All those meetings, I thought we were a team." She laughed out loud while hugging me fiercely. "My brother is having a thing at a lounge downtown. You should come." I shook my head. All I could think about was Shawn. I was all in my head as always. I only wanted to apologize to him. No new men, no old men, only Shawn. "Yes, your coming. I'll be at your place at eight. We have to celebrate tonight!" I looked at her and laughed. "Yes, celebrate to no more meetings that go insanely wrong and toast to new beginnings!" She skipped out my old office with a smile on her face. I sat in my chair for the last time and cut off the desk light. "New beginnings, huh?" I said to no one in particular.

Now You See Me, Now You Don't

* * *

I began my decent down a long flight of steps. My mind was focused on each step, so that I would not trip over my studded heels. I decided to get *dressed* tonight. I had on my backless dress and hair swept up in a high pony tail. I smoothed my dress in the reflection of the window. It was dark outside, but light was illuminating from under the heavy door. Marilyn was singing the song the DJ was playing. She was dressed in low, kitten heels, a pair of dress capris and a halter top. She had a pair of long gold earrings to match her bracelet. We both were scented in **Simple, Delish!** body sprays. I had on *Cherry Goddess* and she, *Turn Up.* Tonight was going to be interesting. The bouncer opened the door, took payment and showed us to the bar. I looked around and noticed two empty seats. When I turned back to ask Marilyn if she wanted to sit there, she was already gone. She was making her way to a table of men that knew her name. I sat at the bar, nursing my diet soda and swaying to the beat. The hairs on my neck began to raise as my mind began to wonder. *I saw Him standing near the balcony, baseball cap in hand, looking out into the night. I was standing next to Shawn with an all white dress* *that left nothing to the imagination. He put his arm around my waist, speaking sweet nothings in my ear. We began to dance at the sounds of the city. The heat of his energy enveloped me in a trance. I wanted to cry, smile, scream and just be. That was how intense his energy drew me in. He brought my mouth closer to his to kiss me when..*"Are you saving this seat?" Shawn stood before me with his eyes wide. I could not read his eyes tonight. He waited for me to move my purse. He didn't smile or show any ounce of knowing who I was. He was standing behind the chair and didn't sit down. I was confused. Until I saw her. She was beautiful, tall and with a head full of curly hair. He pulled out the chair and guided her to the seat. I could feel the heat rise from my belly. I was angry, but had no reason. I did shun him that night, but I wasn't prepared to see this. She asked him for a drink and sat up straight in her chair. She smiled my direction and thanked me for moving my purse. I smiled back. I wanted to get up and move, but then Marilyn came back from the dance floor. She was walking with a gentleman from the table I saw before. She introduced him as Mike. He shook my hand and offered to buy me a drink. "No, I think I am done for the night. Thanks though." I started to put together my items, when I saw Shawn take the stage. He went to the DJ booth and started to play hip hop beats from the nineties. "I can't believe he still likes doing this." The woman he brought with him said loudly. She was finishing her martini. "He is too old to keep trying to pursue this. He has a good job, but he won't give it up." The woman shook her head while rocking in her chair and asked the bartender for another drink. Me and my friend locked eyes, laughing at the sight before us. The woman drank the second drink and began walking toward the door. A man grabbed her hand and walked her outside. I looked up to see Shawn devastated. He locked eyes with me and for a second I could feel his pain. He put down his headphones and rushed out the door after her. I sat back in my chair and registered what happened. *Did she know the guy that she left with?* I thought to myself. But before I could concoct an answer, I saw his devastated face again in my mind. *I would never have done that to him.* I thought to myself, but I could not control what my body did next. I grabbed my purse and headed out the door after Shawn.

In the Blink of an Eye

* * *

I stood back and watched from a far. The woman was holding on to another man as Shawn spoke with her. He was upset, but her anger was more fierce. She rattled off all the things she didn't like about him. She began at his passions, moved forward to his pastimes and landed smack in the middle with his family, all the while, yelling she was not happy with him. He began to yell as well. I tried to listen to his response, but I could not register why she was upset with him. *Why is she mad that he has passions, why is she upset that he spends time with his grandparents on the weekends....why, why, why?* I turned around to see my friend leaving out the door. She was leaving with a gentleman and wanted to see if I could call a taxi to get home. I wanted to be upset, but after watching this event with Shawn, I just shrugged it off. *We will argue about this tomorrow..* I said to myself as Marilyn walked off with her new friend, but not before the woman left with the man she walked out side with. Shawn stood in the middle of the parking lot with his hands in the air. He sensed I was near and turned towards me. "Looks like you got a front role seat." He walked toward me. I looked at him with sadness in my eyes. "Don't feel sorry for me. I was holding on to the idea of *this* getting better. She didn't want me, at least not all of me. And that is her loss...." He looked out over the parking lot as cars drove away. I couldn't find the words to say how I felt. He looked at me and asked a question I would never forget. "If you had to choose between what you loved to do and what you felt would keep the peace, what would you do?" I looked Shawn in his eyes. I saw the Shawn from the other night, the passion, the humor, and the freedom. I remembered just earlier, walking into my bosses office, and resigning without any idea of what was next to come. I remembered all the times I choose to do what others wanted me to do, but never what I wanted. Shawn looked into my eyes deeply, watching intensely while waiting on my answer. Before I could answer, Shawn looked at his watch, straightened up his clothes, and backed away quickly. He went to a gray truck, got in and sped off.

Leaps and Bounds

* * *

Today I woke up with a new feeling. I woke up with the idea that I could do what I wanted to do, how I wanted to do it, just because I wanted to do it. I had no idea where the thought came from, but it was definitely welcomed. I laid there sprawled out over my bed with a smile on my face. The alarm sung my favorite song and I sung with it out loud. My phone rang, but I didn't stop singing. They could wait. As I continued to sing, I heard my answering machine. "Are you there? Are you there? I heard you didn't have a job. Are you there.." I grabbed the phone and said hello. My mother was alarmed and needed reassurance. "Hi mom. I'm okay. I think this is a good change for me. I am doing okay." My mom continued to speak as I began to get ready. Today, I was meeting her at her house. She rescheduled our rendezvous from the other night and I didn't want to be late. "Mom, we can talk about it when I come over there. I have to get dressed." We said our goodbyes and I hurried to jump in the shower. *Today is a good day*, I sang with the clock.

I loved how the trees looked in our old neighborhood. It

reminded me of a nature oasis where you could relax and just be. I got off the shuttle before my stop and decided to walk. I saw a few people from my old high school. One in particular, James, was sitting out in his car when I walked by. "How have you been? I'm sorry about the job. I can see if my company is hiring." James and I hadn't spoke since our ten year reunion. He brought his wife, two kids and dog. The principal advised he couldn't bring in his dog so he took his family home. "I am fine James, but thank you for the offer." He looked at me puzzled. "Its a shame your not married. Your husband could help provide in your tough time." He began shaking his head. One of Jame's daughters came out with her tennis gear. I read in the paper last year that she won quite a few matches and is being considered for scholarships at different prestigious universities across town. "I'm ready to go now." His daughter stated as she threw her bag and racket in their SUV. "It was nice seeing you. I hope you find a job soon." James got in the truck and proceeded to back out of the driveway. I looked down the tree lined street and wondered what life would be like if I was married. *Would he understand my quirkiness or my large imagination? Would he accept my faults and the days I stayed to myself? Would he reciprocate the love I'd give him daily?* I shook my head to dismiss the thoughts I could not answer. I walked toward the house I grew up in. Its door was painted red and white to match the white paint on the fence I climbed as a child. As I reached the driveway, I noticed a truck in the garage. I never saw it there before. Its gray paint was scratched in just the right places. The door handles were silver matching the gray paint on the door. Words were etched into the trucks exterior. "Night Sky". *I wonder what that means,* I thought to myself as I entered my Mothers house. She never locked her door, no matter how many times I fussed. Her front room was airy and painted a soft powder blue. Her plants were positioned on her end tables strategically. The sound of chimes filled the air with suspense and freedom. I loved the scent of coconut that always tinted the air. She loved coconuts, nature and peace and her house reflected it. I found the restroom, but as I closed the door, I heard a familiar voice. "Yes, I love my daughter. She was always the wild child that created in her mind, but on paper she did what every one else did. But her resigning from her job on a whim," my mother shook her head, "well, I'm concerned she is taking things too far..." Her voice trailed off to the kitchen. I heard a second set of footsteps trailing her soft steps. *Who is she talking to?* I thought as I powdered up. I looked for my mother in the kitchen, but I couldn't find her. But who I did lay eyes on took my breathe away. He was sitting on my mothers sofa with one of her favorite mugs in his hand. His baseball cap sat on her table in front on him. His long arms were spread out on the couch as if this wasn't his first time here. I tiptoed past the living room, while my heart ran wild. *Why is Shawn at my mom's house? Why did she tell him about my job?* But before I could come up with a rational explanation, my mother hugged me from behind. "Hey daughter! I missed you!" I turned and wrapped my arms around her small frame. She was a small woman in size but large in life. "Hey mom." We stayed there hugging until a man's voice cleared the air. "Uh um.." He cleared his throat as my mom and I held hands. "Scooter, this is my daughter, Jasmine." *Scooter?* My eyes widened as I broke free from my mother. "Um, how do you know, Scooter?" My eyes danced with Shawn's as I waited for my mother's reply. "You remember, Ann, my friend who owned the corner store on Collins Avenue when you were a child. Well, this is Ann's son, Shawn. Before she went home, I told her that I would keep up with her wonderful son." She grabbed his arm. He held her hand tight. I tried to remember such a beautiful specimen in my past. I went through pictures of students from high school, middle school, and even elementary. Before I began to speak, I remembered a time when I must have been four. I was playing in the yard with a little boy from the neighborhood. He must have pushed me down hard because I still have a slight scar on my knee to this day. I started to cry. I sat there in the dirt crying wildly until a boy older than I brought me to my feet. He wiped my tears and told his friends he would catch up with them. "Ah, your playing with girls!" They screamed and laughed as they ran down the street. The older boy linked our arms and guided me to my mothers house. He opened the door and walked to my mother's sitting room where she sat watching her stories. She began to yell at me for playing with the boys in the neighborhood, but she thanked the little boy. "Thank you Scooter for bringing her in. You can go home now, tell your mom I said, Hi." He un-linked our arms and said goodbye. I never saw him again, no matter how many times I tried to fall in hopes he'd reappear. "Jasmine, there you go again always in your head." My mom shook her head. She was never fond of my daydreams, but they were apart of me like the hair on my head. My mom walked to the sitting room and took a seat. "Now tell me what happened with this job situation.."

Butter Magic

* * *

I began to tell my mother and Shawn the whole story. From the way the managers treated me in the boardroom to the overall communication disparity. I could feel my mom's frustration rise as I poured out my heart. I looked at Shawn who was looking in his hands intensively as if he lost something in them. I sat back fully exhausted by the explanation. I waited for my mother's response. To my surprise, Shawn spoke first. "Do you have a nest egg or a fully stocked savings account?" I knew the answer, but wasn't ready to share. He looked at me as if he understood and read my mind. "Then you have to start hunting before you run out." He leaned back. I finally caught my breathe, still caught in his lingering eyes. "I don't want to go back to that type of environment, it's all the same. When you work hard, they.." My mother interrupted. "Listen to him for once," her eyes trailed to Shawn, "He has been in finance for a long time. He may be able to give you pointers as he did me." She put her hand on his shoulder.

My mother began to tell me how life for her had changed once my father died. I could see the relief in her eyes as she stated it, but was shocked to hear of its truth. You see, my mother wasn't one to tell anyone exactly what was going on. She had a way of making life look better than what it really was. "I was drowning in this mortgage. I took out a second mortgage after your father died and I just couldn't keep up with the payments. I fell behind on the taxes and didn't know what I was going to do." My mom looked to the floor. I could feel the heat rising from my chest. "Why didn't you call me! I could have helped. I could have worked extra projects.." She interrupted, "And have to hear about it later. No ma'am. I raised you and wasn't about to take from you. I'm not elderly yet. Take care of me when I can't do for myself anymore." She waved her hand to dismiss the whole idea. "Anyway, just listen to Shawn. He is very knowledgeable. I asked him to meet you before, but of course, you ran him off." I looked at my mom, then back to Shawn. Then it all began to make sense. "So you were coming to my mom's house the day you were walking me home?" I didn't wait for a reply. "And you knew who I was but you pretended to be a stranger." I couldn't stop speaking. I was livid. "Why did you walk off if you were going to my mom's house? Why did you just leave?" I yelled. My mom stood to cross the room. "Jasmine stop overreacting. Your not thinking clearly. He was only doing me a favor. I wanted him to speak with you about your finances so I arranged for you two to meet at my house. He didn't know you, per say, he had only heard of you." I shook my head. "This is crazy. I thought he was flirting, trying to get to know me, but he was just playing with my head." I threw my hands up. "I'm leaving. Thanks you two, but no thanks!" I stormed out the front door and slammed it shut. I knew I would call my mom to apologize, but at that moment I felt humiliated. Finally I meet a guy who is attractive, his vibe is cool, and his spirit is inviting, but it's a set up from my mom to fix me. *I don't need fixing, I need understanding!* I screamed to no one in particular. I wiped the last tear from my cheek and ran down the street.

Before I Let Go

* * *

My sister called in the wee hours of the morning on the sixteenth. I assumed she was trying to wake me and provide her good news, but I didn't want to hear it. It had been a week since I heard from my mother after apologizing on her answering machine. "Mom, I'm sorry. You know how I am. I just don't need you to try to fix me. Ask me if I need something before assuming I'm broken. I'm not broken mom. Call me back. I love you." She didn't call me back and her answering machine was full. I looked at the clock. *"Three o'clock? Uhhhhh!"* I sighed out loud and put the pillow over my head.

We held each other while looking over the town. The perch was on a mountain top, I'd never been to before. He always found the most picturesque places to take me. He grabbed my hand and kissed my fingers so gingerly, so gently. "I love you," he said in a sexy, masculine voice. He pulled me closer. The smell of his **Deep Earth** Beard Oil tickled my senses and shot electricity down my spine. I wanted him, right then, right there. He pulled me closer. I could feel his breathing as he kissed my neck. He blew on my neck with a cool, steady flow of air, while telling me how beautiful I was. He slid his hand to the small of my back. I looked into his eyes, yearning for him to put my passion to its misery. He slowly dropped the spaghetti strap of my dress when…"BEEP. ITS TIME TO RISE..BEEP." I screamed in agony for I was almost to a place of ecstasy in my dream. I shook my head. "If only I could have the real thing!" I yelled out loud. I stood as my phone rang. It was my sister, again.

A moment is Forever

* * *

As my sister spoke her words, I could feel my body become limp and fall to the floor. My mother had been so upset the night of our fight that she pranced the floor speaking with Shawn. She thanked him for coming and for listening but before she could close the door, she fell to the floor. Shawn called the ambulance. She was taken to the county hospital near her house. I listened as my sister cried through the phone. My blood began to boil. "Why didn't he call us? Why didn't Shawn make us aware?" Mia hesitated as she answered. I grabbed a pair of leggings and a sweatshirt and quickly began dressing. Mia began to speak. "She told him not to trouble us because we have our own issues going on..." Her voice trailed. I threw my phone as I cried out loud. "Why does she assume she's not worthy of our love? Look what she has done for us for so many years." I grabbed my shoes and my phone off the floor. "Jasmine, she means well. She just didn't want us to worry." Mia tried to explain. I wrote down the hospital address and headed to the door.

"I am here to see Evelyn-" I spoke to a nurse at the nursing station, but I looked over and saw Shawn sitting on a bench. His head was in hands as he sat next to someone. I went to him and asked what room my mom was in. He mentioned she just got out of surgery, but gave the number 414. Before he could mention any details, I ran to find her room. To my surprise, he caught up with me just before I found her room. Shawn pulled me towards him and hugged me close. I could feel his energy calming me. He looked into my eyes and said something to my soul that put my mind at ease. He politely kissed my cheek and opened the door to my mom's room. All the anger I felt from this morning towards my mom washed away. I saw a frail woman in a hospital gown who slept peacefully on her side. I sat down in the chair next to my mom's bed. I could hear her breathing slowly as I watched her chest rise and fall. I felt Shawn's eyes on me from the door before he walked away. "Jasmine." My mom quietly spoke while turning her body. She clenched as she moved. "Don't move mom; let me help you." I helped her position her head higher on the pillow and lay on her back. Her face and lip were bruised from the fall, but her eyes were still bright and alive. "You shouldn't have come...", my mom began to exclaim. I cut her off and began to cry. "I can and will be here for you, no matter what. And there is nothing you can do about it..." My voice trailed off as I hugged my mother's small frame. I rocked her for what felt like hours until her nurse came in for test. They advised that her visiting hours were over, but I could come as early as I wanted. I tried to contest it, but my mother shook her head to silence me. I blew her a kiss, gathered my items, and walked into the hallway.

Hours felt like days as I sat on the hard chairs of the hospital waiting room. I was waiting for my sister when Shawn appeared with food. He smiled as he laid eyes on me and made his way to the seat next to me. "Do you want chicken or turkey?" I motioned for the chicken. He unwrapped the sandwich, laid out condiments and put a straw in the boxed water. "Thank you for being so nice Shawn. I can't say I deserve it." I stuffed my mouth with the cold, chicken sandwich. He sat back in his seat and put mayonnaise on his sandwich. He smiled as he looked my way. "Whose to say I'm deserving of your company?" He shrugged as he drank his water. I shook my head and thought, *why the riddles?* I looked up to see my sister and her fiance coming through the front door. She held her purse on her wrist and he held her other hand. They looked like stars even in this hospital setting. "Jasmine, Shawn." She smiled a sinister smile. "We went ahead and booked two rooms right next door so we can be close to mom. Here is your key and room info." I looked at my sister and gave her a confused look. "Is this for one room or two?" I looked at Shawn who looked ambiguous. "Jasmine, two grown people can share a hotel room. Get some rest. We'll talk in the morning." Before I could speak my peace, Mia sashayed out the door with her man in tow.

All This Love

* * *

Someone once told me, "Always make sure your under garments matched and were free of discrepancies," and I am truly happy for that peace of information. I slowly dressed while sitting on the bed. I wasn't prepared for this hotel trip, but was glad to hand wash my items. I bathed as soon as we got into the room to avoid having to stare at his gorgeous face. He was taking a shower. I tried to decide how to lay on the bed. *"Do I lay with my head up here as his head is down there? Do we lay the same way with me on top of the sheets and him underneath the sheets or do I lay on the chair and call it a night?"* I wrestled with those thoughts when he opened the door and took my breath away. Now I'm not one to fall in love with the way a person looks, but my mind, body, and soul fell in love with his aura instantly. He tightened his towel and sat on the bed. He smelled of Ripped Body Oils from **Deep Earth** and looked like a heavenly sculptured creation. His back was toward me, as he focused on his clothing. I could see his muscles flex as he put his tee shirt over his head and rolled it down his abs. My mind was on fire and knew I would have a major tongue lashing with my sister in the morning. She was one to set up the most unique situations, but I wasn't fond of her not forewarning me. Shawn put his towel away and laid under the covers. My body felt weak as my eyes scanned his gorgeous, chocolate body. He politely motioned for me to come lay next to him. I climbed under the covers to feel the warmth of a man next to me. His legs were toned and felt like strength. Before I could imagine how this night could get any better, he pulled me close to him, wrapped his long arms around me and whispered, "Goodnight", in my ear. I could do nothing but melt in his arms as we both drifted off to sleep.

When the Moon and Stars Collide

* * *

I realized I wasn't one for daydreaming all day, but as I sat up to start my day, my mind couldn't let the events from last week go. My mother was doing better and I annoyed her by calling her daily to check on her. She said she was supposed to check on me, but the roles were reversed. I have been by her side as she worked through her recovery process. I found the newspaper on my desk as I read through the unemployment opportunities. *Looking for a great self starter, a goal setter, and a lover of people,* I shook my head as I threw the paper on my bed. I gathered my items to take a shower. I would be heading out to meet Mia soon. She'd be waiting on the bench at our favorite park cursing to the trees. "She is never on time...", she'd tell no one in particular as she looked at her watch. My sister was predictable, but I loved her no less.

The water cascaded down my frame as I closed my eyes. I could feel heat rising on my back as he kissed me with slow, gentle kisses. He found his way to my ear as he spoke about the love and passion he had for me. He expressed he wanted to show me his love instead of telling me. He gently turned my face toward his, kissing my lips with soft, yet strong kisses. I moaned at the way he caressed my face with his hand while looking deep into his soul. My mind began to wonder if I would finally experience a volcanic eruption when... "RING, RING", the doorbell sounded. I wiped my eyes and noticed how heavily steamed the shower door was. I laughed at the heat rising from my skin. I rinsed and put on my light pink robe. "Coming!" I yelled as hurried to the door, not noticing my damp curls on my shoulders. It was cool in the house by the breeze from the window. I finally opened the door, and was greeted by the doorman of my building. He carried a bouquet of flowers that stopped me in my tracks. They were white with pink petals that smelled of Jasmine. I frowned at the smiling doormen perched the flowers in my hands. "These came in for you today." His smile brightened the hallway. I stood back looking hard at the flowers as my heart skipped a beat. I grabbed the card and read the note out loud. "Time will not keep us apart. I found you, yet again. Michael." I dropped the flowers on the floor and backed into the apartment. I closed the door and as the doorman knocked again and again, I slid down to the floor with my head in my hands.

You Can Run, but You Can't Hide

* * *

"I can't believe this," I spoke swiftly to my already frustrated sister. She sat with her hands in her lap and her mouth pursed tightly. She waited an hour for me to show up and was having a hard time understanding my distress. "But you two were high school sweethearts right?" She stated annoyed. I stood to adjust my jacket. The evening had a breeze that sent chills down my spine. I looked over the rail into the river that ran along the side the park. Riverside was one of the nicest parks in the city. From the tree lined sidewalks to the view of the river, it was were families and couples alike came to relax and unwind. I sat down and remembered *our* time here as well.

He was running late, but he made an entrance I would never forget. He had a bouquet of white flowers with pink petals. He slid between me and the river vying for my attention. I smiled as he danced with the flowers before handing them to me. They smelled delicious. We had come here more times than I could count. We would joke around, bring lunch and sit on the grass or walk hand and hand down the sidewalk. This time I

35

hoped it would be different. We had dated for five years, never missing a beat. We talked about marriage and children someday soon. Moments before, he called and said he had something very important to tell me. I got dressed as soon as possible and hurried to see him. As I held the beautiful flowers, I awaited those magical words to end the night. He took my hand and brought me to the nearby bench. "Jasmine, you know I love you and there is nothing I wouldn't do for you. Lately, I've been thinking about our lives and what I want to do. I want to pursue a trucking business. I know this is new, but hear me out. I also want to explore the new feelings that have been developing..." His voice trailed on as I processed his words. "Are you breaking up with me?" I tried to keep my tears from falling. "It's great you have a new career interest. We can do that together." I tried to speak quickly and calmly. He shook his head and stood to his feet. "You always do this. This is about me, not you. I want to pursue my career, but I don't want you to benefit from it. I've fallen in love with someone else and she doesn't make me feel bad for the changes I want to make. She gets me." He had a smug smile on his face. I slapped his face hard. Near by walkers looked our directions and scurried off. He touched his face and spit. "How dare you? We've been through thick and thin together for the past five years. What about when your father past? I was right there to help you pick up the pieces. I went with you to therapy when you wanted to quit taking pills. I was there helping you when you decided to change your job last year, creating your resume and answering your emails. What else can I do to prove to you I'm a great woman for you?" I put my head in my hands and began to sob. My heart cracked in many pieces as I tried to take in air. *How could he want to leave after all I've done for him?* I hoped he was having a change of heart, but was quickly brought back to reality. I looked into his eyes and saw a cold, loveless man. A man that I never met before. He stuck his hands in his pocket and shifted another direction. "I'll be there to get my clothes in the morning. I'm staying at Sandy's house tonight. It's not you, Jasmine it's me..." He walked off toward the entrance of the park. I let out a loud wail as I watched him walk away. I couldn't understand why I never saw his distress with me, his disdain of me before this day. I tried to scan the many dates, nights we talked and could not find a reason for his dismissal. I slowly got to my feet and wiped my face. A young girl clang to her mother as she watched me attempt to walk towards my car. I opened up my door and found a check written nicely on my seat with a note. *This should cover the last five years I've lived at your house and borrowed your car. Don't worry, you don't have to thank me.* I threw the check and beat the steering wheel while screaming to the top of my lungs.

I tried to explain to my sister how his betrayal shaped the next years of my dating life. But each time I spoke, she shook her head. "He sent me those flowers to try to get me back. But I no longer want him. He is my past." I stood up and walked to the railing. My sister stood and walked next to me. "I get it, Jasmine. He was a douche bag before, but maybe you guys can meet to determine if you are truly over him. A sort of final goodbye." She put her her arm around my shoulder. I leaned into the arms of my sister. Tears fell as she wiped them away. Birds began to chirp as the day escaped us. "He left this check on my car seat years ago..." My voice trailed on. She studied the check and gave a wide smile. "All the more reason to go out and eat tonight. Bills on him!" We both laughed a long hearty laugh before heading to our cars.

Jokes On You

* * *

The Japanese spot was packed tonight. All the couples were child free and dressed to the T. We could barely find parking at this once empty restaurant. We have been going here for quite a while. *The Wok'ing* began with one waitress, Sadie and one chef named Wonn. They were a husband and wife powerhouse who loved people and expensive Sake'. My sister and I would joke with them on the slowest of days, taking the stress out of having only one table booked. But look at them now. New management, waitstaff, hostess, packed establishment and a large dance floor gave the restaurant a very hip vibe. Sadie and Wonn didn't work in the restaurant any longer. They only checked in on staff monthly. We took our favorite table in the front corner and waited for the wait staff. "Jasmine you have a decision to make. If you take my advice, and yes you should, you should reach out to Michael to set up a lunch date to discuss his thoughts. You can then choose what to do afterwards. The ball would be in your court." My sister sat back in her chair as if she just gave the State of the Union speech. I shook my head as the waitress came to take our orders. Mia got her usual strawberry tea and for me I asked for red wine. Today really deserved such a drink. As the waitress, Alee, walked away, I excused myself to powder up. I felt uneasy as I walked past the tables and bar. I wasn't sure if I was hungry or needed to sit down. But then I heard two very familiar voices speaking with each other and I felt like I was going to fall promptly to the floor. I froze and listened intently.

"Here is a picture of her, " Michael stated matter of factly as he showed his new business partner. "We dated for years, but I needed a break to see what else was out there." His voice was smug. "Yeah, I'm ready to get her back, so I sent her some roses. She can't resist them." Michael sat back in his seat with a sly smile. He looked at Shawn who sat with his arms folded. He was nursing a tea and hot Misoshiru. I was able to move out of the servers way as Michael spoke, but I couldn't breathe waiting on Shawn's response. "What if she doesn't want to take you back?" Shawn raised his eyebrows as he peered at Michael. "Oh, she'll take me back. We were together for five years. She hasn't even dated since our break up. I've seen her around town with her sister Mia. She's lonely and waiting on my touch." Michael laughed and finished his lager. I tried to stretch and see Shawn's physical response, when a waitress holding two large trays lost control while trying to pass me. She dropped the plates and ran for help. I stood there looking around as those eating their meals looked at me with disdain. "I didn't do anything," I told no one in particular, but to all who watched. I tried to pick up as many dishes as I could but was bombarded by the cleaning staff. They pushed me out the way and began to clean the mess. As I turned to go back to my table, my eyes locked with Shawn's. He looked scrumptious. I hurried back to my table only to see

Michael sitting in my seat talking with Mia. She was laughing at his jokes and allowing him to woo her. I took a sharp turn and hurried out of the restaurant. I found a seat near the front and allowed the wind to fill my lungs. "It's a great night to take in the night sky." Shawn walked my way. He always took my breathe away. "Yeah, I'm in need of it right now." I crossed my arms as the wind blew. "I figured the wine on the table was yours, so I got us both one." Shawn gave me a glass and sat next to me. I closed my eyes and inhaled his mesmerizing scent of Coconut and Tobacco, an oil by **Deep Earth**. What I didn't know was that he was also allured by the scented oil of Sensuality, by ***Simple, Delish!*** that I had placed on my wrist and behind my ears. When I opened my eyes, the view took my breathe away. Shawn enveloped my face in his hands and kissed me so soft, but firm. He breathed in my tears, my anxiety and stresses of the night and released a strong breath of peace. His eyes told me secrets I'd never heard before and I agreed to his want and desire. Before I could say a word, he stood, kissed my forehead and turned to walk off. I could not believe he was leaving me after such an intense kiss. As I put my head in my hands, I felt the stare of someone. I looked up and saw Shawn's hand out, waiting on me to take it. I stood, but heard laughter. I looked the other way to see Mia and Michael coming out of the restaurant. "Jasmine what are you doing out here....." Her voice trailed off as she saw Shawn's hand waiting on my response. I moved toward Shawn slowly when I heard Michael speak. "Ah, so you're trying to take Jasmine away Shawn? You thought you could after what I told you?" Michael laughed out loud. "I wouldn't do that if I was you, Jasmine. I know his past and present. Much of which, you don't." Michael rubbed his hands to together and began to smile. "Let's start with the beginning, shall we. Shawn is married..." I looked at Shawn. His neck muscles flexed and his eyes sent out a blaze. He backed away from my hand as I looked at him with confusion. He took off swiftly in the direction of his truck. "Shawn is it true?" I yelled as I walked his direction hoping to catch up with him. He pulled the truck handle and stopped in his tracks. I touched his hand as he looked at the door of his grey truck. He breathed deeply as if it hurt him. Shawn sighed a long sigh while shaking his head. I began to go into my head trying to make up a scenario that would end with me happily in his arms. As I tried to believe my thoughts, his voice woke me from my daydream. He spoke the words I wish I never heard, "Yes."

To be continued....

More From Kiamani Robey

Want more *enticing fiction*? Catch sultry short stories that will fill your desire for great fiction on Spotify, titled, *Adult Bedtime Stories for the Creative Soul* by Kiamani Robey. https://open.spotify.com/episode/5HL2wKpZMZ9wrlcwnwJCMc

Connect on social media:

Twitter.com/@simpledelish

Instagram.com/thesimpledelish

Facebook.com/kiamani.robey.3

Epilogue

"Shawn, is it true?"

She asked while coming towards me. I looked at my truck door. I took a lot of time redesigning and sanding it, to make it the door it was. Carpentry and finance were two of my most lucrative professions, but I liked to refurbish antique cars and trucks for sport. Jasmine put her hand on mine as my mind raced. *How could I tell her what happened without her running away? Will she want to know my truth?* I breathed deeply and responded to her, "Yes." She removed her hand and backed away. I saw her face in the mirror, scrunched up with distress. I turned to try to touch her, but she ran back to her sister and my low down business partner, Michael. I shook off my feelings and started my truck. It started loudly with the hard work of many years toil. I loved my truck, but not as much as I loved Jasmine. But right then she wasn't ready to know. She also wasn't ready for me. I backed out of the parking space and drove off in rare form.

Excerpted from: *In Between a Rock & a Hard Place*, sequel to *Shea Butter Rocks by:* Kiamani Robey

About the Author

Kiamani Robey was born June 8, 1983 in Columbus, Ohio. She and her family moved to Jackson, Mississippi when she was 9 and ended up in Atlanta, Georgia her second year in high school. Robey has been an up and coming writer since 1997. Robey won numerous awards including a Poetry Badge for Young Adults. Robey continued her writing through blog creation, including the Value of Beauty, where she breaks down the definition of beauty and its power. Robey continued her writing journey with the creation of the Love Your Health podcast. This podcast spotlights healthy choices for individuals, including mental and physical improvement. She also completed her first book in the Healthy Living Series, Seven Steps Toward Healthy Living. This book is a step by step process for individuals on their healthy living journey, where they can begin goal preparation, tackle process formation, and completion. Robey has continued her writing journey with Take Me As I Am, the second book of her Healthy Living Series. It is a compelling combination of straightforward ideas that keep readers on their toes. Its interactive non-fiction theme presents deep questions to keep the reader engaged and compelled to complete the next chapter. Robey has also created a companion guide to help guide the reader through tough question and answer sessions. Robey is now embarking on a fictional journey with Shea Butter Rocks and the rest of the love inspired series. Be on the look out!

You can connect with me on:

🌐 https://simpledelish.wixsite.com/valueofbeauty

Also by Kiamani Robey

The journey to healthy living doesn't have to be daunting. If you are ready for a step by step process and a chance to get "real" with your past, present and/or future, while preserving your truth, read these books by Kiamani Robey. Book one and two of the Healthy Living Series.

Seven Steps Toward Healthy Living

Want to start your journey on healthy living? Get Seven Steps Toward Healthy Living by Kiamani Robey. Available on Amazon.

Take Me As I Am

Have you ever dreamed of clearing cobwebs of the past in an easy way? Purchase Take Me As I Am by Kiamani Robey. Now available on Amazon and Barnes and Noble.

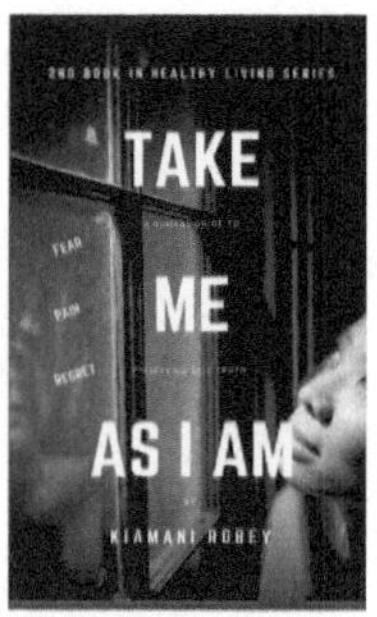

Take Me As I Am Companion Workbook
Achieve your dreams by challenging your inner thoughts, ideas with Kiamani Robey's Companion Workbook. Available on Amazon and Barnes and Noble.